Laura Valentine, Joseph Martin Kronheim, Kate Greenaway

Aunt Louisa's nursery favourite

Laura Valentine, Joseph Martin Kronheim, Kate Greenaway

Aunt Louisa's nursery favourite

ISBN/EAN: 9783743376953

Manufactured in Europe, USA, Canada, Australia, Japa

Cover: Foto ©Andreas Hilbeck / pixelio.de

Manufactured and distributed by brebook publishing software (www.brebook.com)

Laura Valentine, Joseph Martin Kronheim, Kate Greenaway

Aunt Louisa's nursery favourite

AUNT LOUISA'S

NURSERY FAVOURITE.

COMPRISING

Diamonds and Toads.   Lily Sweetbriar.

Dick Whittington.   Uncle's Farm Yard.

WITH

TWENTY-FOUR PAGES OF ILLUSTRATIONS.

Printed in Colours by Kronheim.

LONDON:

FREDERICK WARNE AND CO.

BEDFORD STREET, COVENT GARDEN.

NEW YORK: SCRIBNER, WELFORD AND CO.

1870.

PREFACE.

THE Publishers of the "AUNT LOUISA's" Toy Books offer a New Volume to their young readers, containing old and new Stories. It is hoped that DIAMONDS AND TOADS, and DICK WHITTINGTON, may please in their new garb; and that LILY SWEETBRIAR and the rural scenes which render Farm life so delightful to children, may render the book worthy of the title of the "Nursery Favourite."

LONDON, BEDFORD STREET, COVENT GARDEN.

DIAMONDS AND TOADS.

DIAMONDS AND TOADS.

ONCE upon a time, in the days of the Fairies, there lived, on the borders of a great wood, a widow who had two daughters. She was a silly, ill-tempered woman, very proud and disagreeable. Her elder daughter, who was like her in temper, was her favourite child; and she spoiled her by constant praise and petting, till the girl grew so proud and rude, that no one loved her except her mother. The younger daughter was sweet-tempered, gentle, and kind; but her foolish mother did not love her, and treated her very unkindly. She made her live in the kitchen, and work all day with the servants. One of the girl's tasks was to draw water twice a day from a fountain, more than a mile and a half distant from the house, in the midst of the wood. One day, just as she had filled her pitcher, an old woman came up to her, and asked her to give her a draught of water.

Diamonds and Toads.

"Willingly, Goody," replied the girl. "Let me hold the jug for you, for it is very heavy."

As soon as the old dame had finished drinking, she said to Rose,

"Thank you, my dear; you are so kind, and you speak so sweetly, that I mean to bestow a gift on you. Every time you speak there shall drop from your lips a rose, a diamond, and a pearl."

Then the old woman disappeared. She was really a Fairy in disguise, who had wished to try whether the young girl was civil and kind.

When Rose reached her home, her mother met her at the door, and began to scold her for staying so long at the fountain.

"I am very sorry: I beg your pardon, mother," she said meekly, "for not coming home sooner." And as she spoke there fell from her lips two pearls, three diamonds, and two roses.

"What do I see? what is this?" cried the mother; "she drops diamonds and pearls from her lips! My child"—(this was the first time that she had ever called her "my child")—"how did this happen?"

2

Diamonds and Toads.

Then the poor girl told her mother all that had befallen her at the fountain, dropping pearls and diamonds from her mouth all the time she was speaking.

How very fortunate!" said the old lady: "I must send my darling thither directly. Fanny! do you see what falls from your sister's lips when she speaks? Should you not like such a gift? Well, you must go to the fountain, and when a poor woman asks you for water, you must grant her request in the most civil manner."

"Indeed," answered the proud girl, "I shall do no such thing. I do not choose to be servant to any one."

"But you *shall* go," said her mother; and for once she made her disobedient child obey her. But Fanny took the best silver tankard, instead of the brown pitcher.

She had no sooner reached the fountain, than a lady most magnificently dressed came out of the woodland path, and asked Fanny to give her some water. This was the same Fairy who had before appeared as a poor old woman; and she came for the same purpose, that was, to try whether the young girl was kind and obliging; but

3

lest she should only pretend goodness in order to gain the precious gift, the Fairy appeared in a different form.

"I did not come here to draw water for strangers," said Fanny, scornfully; "I suppose you think the best silver tankard was brought on purpose for *your* ladyship! However, you may drink out of it if you have a fancy."

"You are not very obliging," said the Fairy; "and since you have behaved with so little civility, I will bestow a gift on *you* which shall be your punishment. Every time you speak, there shall drop from your lips a viper or a toad."

Having said these words she disappeared; and Fanny went home very sullen and angry. As soon as her mother saw her coming, she ran to meet her, and exclaimed eagerly,

"Well, daughter?"

"Well, mother," answered the girl, and two toads and two vipers dropped from her mouth as she spoke!

"Ah-h-h! what is this?" cried the mother; "it is all your sister's doing, no doubt. *I*'ll make her suffer for her wickedness!"

4

And she instantly went in search of the poor innocent girl, that she might beat her severely.

But Rose, in great fear, ran out of the house into the forest, where she wandered about, weeping very bitterly. Towards evening, the King's son, who was returning from hunting, came that way, and seeing a poor girl apparently in great trouble, he alighted from his horse, and asked her why she wept; for he was very kind and good-hearted.

"Alas!" said Rose, sobbing, "my mother is so cruel to me that I have been obliged to leave my home."

The King's son was astonished to see roses, pearls, and diamonds fall from her lips as she spoke, and asked her the reason of such a wonder. The girl then related all that had befallen her at the fountain. The Prince was charmed with her innocence and gentleness, and fell in love with her. He saw that, although she was only a poor girl, she possessed a valuable gift which would make him and his people very rich; so he took her back to the palace of the King his father, who, anxious to have such a daughter-in-law, im-

mediately gave his consent to their marriage, and the gentle Rose became a great Queen.

As for her sister, the toads and vipers she dropped were so dreadful, that her selfish and cruel mother soon grew tired of having her in the house, and turned her out of doors. As she had not improved, but was worse tempered than ever, no one would take her in, and be troubled with toads and vipers. So she was obliged to wander about in the woods, all alone; and there she soon died of grief and hunger.

Kind words are as precious as pearls and diamonds, and as sweet as roses. Cross, unkind words are as bad as toads and vipers.

DICK WHITTINGTON.

THE OLD BALLAD

OF

DICK WHITTINGTON.

 MERCHANT once upon a time, who had great store of
gold,
Among his household placed a youth sore pinch'd by want and cold;
No father or no mother watch'd with love o'er this poor boy,
Whose dearest treasure was a Cat, his pet and only joy,
That came to him beseechingly when death was at the door,
And kindly to relieve her wants he shared his little store.
A grateful Cat! no mice might live where she put up to dwell,
And Whittington could calmly sleep, while Puss watched o'er his
cell,
That once o'erran with vermin so, no rest had he by night,
Placed in this garret vile to please a cruel woman's spite.

1

Alice advises him to send his Cat.

Now on the Thames a gallant ship lay ready to set sail,
When spoke the Merchant, "Ho! prepare to catch the fav'ring
    gale;
And each who will his fortune try, haste, get your goods on board,
The gains ye all shall share with me, whate'er they may afford;
From distant lands where precious musks and jewels rare are
    found,
What joy to waft across the seas their spoils to English ground!"
So hasted then each one on board, with what he best could find,
Before the ship for Afric's land flew swiftly with the wind.
The little boy he was so poor, no goods had he to try,
And as he stood and saw the ship, a tear bedimm'd his eye,
To think how Fortune smiled on all except on his sad lot—
As if he were by gracious Heaven neglected and forgot!
The Merchant and his daughter too, fair Alice, mark'd his grief,
And with a gentle woman's heart, intent on kind relief,
She bade him bring his Cat to try her fortune o'er the sea;
"Who knows," she said, "what she may catch in gratitude to
    thee!"
With weeping and with sore lament he brought poor Puss on board;
And now the ship stood out for sea, with England's produce
    stored.

Hearing Bells.

And as she sped far out of sight, his heart was like to break;
His friend had gone that shared his crust, far sweeter for her sake.
Humble his lot the Merchant knew, but knew not that the Cook
With blows and cuffs the boy assail'd, and surly word and look;
Until his life a burden seemed, too grievous to be borne,
Though Alice oft would pity him, so lowly and forlorn.
Now musing long, the thought arose his plight could scarce be
    worse,
And forth he rush'd into the fields, regardless of his course.
The cutting winds blew bleak and cold upon his shiv'ring breast,
His naked feet were pierced with thorns, on every side distress'd;
He sank, o'erpowered with grief and pain, upon a wayside stone,
Bethinking there to end his days, with none to make him moan:
And calling upon God for aid in this last hour of need—
On God, who never yet refused to hear the wretched plead.
And now the bells sound loud and clear, as thus he lay forlorn,
Seeming to say, "O Whittington, thou foolish boy, return!
Lord Mayor of London thou shalt be, Dick Whittington, if thou
Wilt turn again, and meet thy lot with bold and manly brow."*

---

* The six bells of Bow Church rung, and seemed to say to him:

"Turn again, Whittington, Lord Mayor of London;
Turn again, Whittington, Lord Mayor of London."

3

Up sprang the boy to hear such sounds, so cheerful and so
    sweet,

He felt no more the piercing winds, the thorns beneath his feet,

But raising up his eyes to Heaven, he prayed for strength to
    bear

Whatever in His wisdom God might please to make him share.

And now his steps retracing fast, good news he quickly hears,

How that a richly-laden ship, amid ten thousand cheers,

Had enter'd port from distant climes full freighted with their
    gold,

By traffic gain'd for English wares in honest barter sold.

With shout and song the crew rejoiced — not less the folk on
    shore—

Told of adventures strange and rare among the blackamoor;

And how their King was glad to see our English sailors bold,

Who sat and ate and drank with him from cups of purest gold.

Once on a day, amid their cheer, when healths went gaily round,

How were the crew amazed to see, in swarms upon the ground,

Unnumber'd rats and mice rush forth and seize the goodly
    cheer,

While stood the wond'ring guests aloof, o'erwhelmed with dread
    and fear.

Cat at Banquet Killing Rats.

"Oh!" said the King, "what sums I'd give to rid me of these vile

Detested rats, whose ravages our bed and board defile!"

Now hearing this, the sailors straight bethought them of the Cat,

And said, "O King, we'll quickly rid your palace of each rat."

"Indeed!" the King delighted said; "go fetch her, quick as thought,

For such a treasure, many a year, I've long and vainly sought;

And should she prove as ye have said, your ship shall loaded be

With gold in heaps, so rich a prize I deem your Cat to be."

And now the Cat did soon perform such feats as ne'er were seen;

Oh, how the scampering, mangled rats amused the King and Queen!

Rich treasures now for Whittington were sent on board the ship,

That, laden with a golden freight, did let her cables slip,

And stood for England, while the breeze a fav'ring impulse lent,

As if for sake of Whittington both ship and breeze were sent.

And soon again the bells rang forth a loud and merry strain,

For wealth and honours crowded now on Whittington amain:

The Marriage.

With gentle Alice for his bride, he stands before the priest,
And after holy rites and vows comes next the wedding feast.
The poor were feasted well, I ween, upon that happy day,
And never from his door did go the poor uncheer'd away.
"Lord Mayor of London" spoke the bells—they spoke both well
    and true;
And still the stone is pointed out unto the traveller's view,
Where Whittington, in prayer to God, cast all his fears aside,
And rose and braced him for the strife, whatever might betide.

LILY SWEETBRIAR.

LILY SWEETBRIAR'S BIRTHDAY.

HAVE known many dear little people,
  And num'rous the charms they possess'd;
But bright little Lily Sweetbriar
  I ever loved dearest and best.

A child fond of frolic and sunshine,
  A wee, winsome, mischievous elf;
Yet gentle, and loving, and kindly,
  She thought very little of self.

She came when the snowdrops were nodding
  O'er violets timid and sweet;
When pert little crocus looked daring,
  And laughed at the cold driving sleet.

Dear reader, you've oft seen a sunbeam
  Glide into a dark dingy room,
And spread light and warmth by its presence,
  Where all had been chillness and gloom?

Thus a child with a bright cheerful spirit
  Sheds pleasure and gladness around,
In the home of the peer or the peasant,
  Wherever its light may be found.

Papa was quite proud of his Lily;
  And when her next birthday drew near,
Told Mamma to invite a large party,
  For music, and games, and good cheer.

1

Lily's eyes shone like two little planets
  When she heard the resolve of Papa,
And off to the nurs'ry she scamper'd,
  To relate the consent of Mamma.

Papa then produced a neat inkstand,
  Mamma brought a golden-nibbed pen;
Lily sat down to write invitations,
  "Tea at six, and the supper at ten."

Old Time cannot run any faster
  For our birthdays, wish it as we may;
He has too many matters to settle,
  In his twelve working hours per day.

But at last dawned the longed-for morning,
  And Lily woke up in delight;
The first thing that entered her wise head
  Was "My birthday, and party to-night!"

The first to arrive was Aunt Susan,
  Pale, pensive, and quiet, and fair;
She brought a pearl locket for Lily;
  Inside was a piece of her hair.

And while she bestowed it, dear Auntie
  Breath'd over her darling a pray'r,
"The Pearl of Great Price might be Lily's,
  To keep her soul spotless and fair."

The next was Aunt Florence, the widow,
  So calm and so sweetly resigned;
To know her was surely to love her,
  So cheerful, so thoughtful, so kind.

2

A warm kiss she gave to dear Lily,
  With a book bound in crimson and gold,
And murmur'd a pray'r that her darling
  Might be good, both when young and when old.

And then Cousin Hector, the soldier,
  All bombast, moustachios, and scent,
With a speech wherein nonsense abounded,
  Presented a watch made by Dent.

And young Cousin Emma, the orphan,
  Gave a purse made of blue silk and beads,
With a hope its contents might be always
  Spent on kindly and generous deeds.

Next, pale Cousin Edward, the poet,
  Brought a rose and a most melting lay,
Written all about Truth, Love, and Beauty;
  Just fit for the child and the day.

Now, brave Cousin Hal, the young sailor,
  Just returned from the perilous sea,
Had jotted before in his "Log-book,"
  "Cousin Lily" and "Music and tea."

He brought two green birds from Australia,
  A curious box from Japan,
A queer little idol from China,
  And a lovely carved ivory fan.

On Bachelor Ben, the rich Uncle,
  Red and portly, and brim-full of fun,
Ev'ry face in the room beam'd a welcome;
  Mamma said, "So glad you are come!"

.

After answering all the kind greetings,
  He held up his arm in the air,
And begg'd those who were present to notice
  That not one sleeve-button was there!

Then he called aloud for Niece Lily,
  And declared he'd his darling disown
If she did not the very next minute
  Sew the buttons, now wanting, all on.

"Oh, Uncle," said poor little Lily,
  "You can't be in earnest, I know!
'Tis my birthday; I haven't my work-box;
  You surely don't want me to sew?"

"Come hither, you pert little monkey,"
  He said with a shake of his head,
And drew out a beautiful housewife,
  Full of buttons, and needles, and thread.

Poor Lily could hardly help crying;
  But she knew that she must not be rude,
So at once did her best by complying
  With her Uncle Ben's whimsical mood.

Hal's blue eyes then opened still wider,—
  He thought her a fairy outright;
But I think both the soldier and poet
  Were a "leetle bit" shocked at the sight.

Uncle Ben gave her cheek a sly pinching,
  And then a good warm hearty kiss;
And Lily's sweet smile gave assurance
  His joke was not taken amiss.

4

At last Uncle John, the young curate,
　Came in, looking pale and careworn;
He had worked for the service of others
　Till eve from the earliest morn.

And now he had come from a night-school;
　It had once been a mere robbers' den;
Where he tried hard to turn boyish vagrants
　Into honest and hard-working men.

He said he need not, for late coming,
　Apology make, he well knew;
Then smilingly, from his coat-pocket,
　A purple-bound volume he drew.

He said, with a look at dear Lily,
　"Dont fear, I am not going to preach;
My gift if you ponder it duly,
　Your duty, my darling, will teach.

"Take this book, my dear girl, for your guide,
　Companion, and counsellor sweet;
May its honey still sweeten your life,
　Its lamp be a light to your feet.

"Drink often at Wisdom's pure fountain,
　Weigh all in her balance of gold;
She has rubies and treasures to give you,
　Whose value have never been told.

"Seek her early, and she will be with you,
　Imparting a beauty divine;
For they only who walk in her footsteps,
　In true and pure loveliness shine."

Now came supper, and afterwards parting,
  Warm wraps, and looks out at the sky;
Little laughs, kisses sweet, and good wishes;
  And then the last cab, and "good bye."

And then little Lily, quite tired,
  Was left to her presents and dreams,
In which green birds changed into squirrels,
  Her rose into cakes and ice creams.

They talk of the gifts of the Fairies,
  The presents Queen Mab often brings;
But, to me, aunts, uncles, and cousins,
  Are by far the more sensible things.

I fear that some dear little reader
  Is now very likely to cry,
"I am not in the least like your Lily,—
  No presents for me my friends buy."

Come here, lay your head on my bosom;
  This is but one day in a life;
For twenty of feasting and pleasure,
  There are hundreds of struggle and strife.

We are not made only for pleasure:
  Our life is a nursery, a school,
Where presents and parties come seldom,
  And happiness is not the rule.

Strive first to be useful, then happy,—
  I know that the roses will bloom;
But there must be labour and waiting
  Ere the ripe sheaves are carried safe home.

UNCLE'S FARM YARD.

UNCLE'S FARM-YARD.

IT was on a fine sunshiny afternoon, that Mary, and I (Harry Pitt) and little Annie, arrived at Uncle John's Farm, on our long visit. I think it would not be possible to find a prettier house than Clayfield is. It is very old; there are great beams of wood in the brickwork of the walls outside, which I never saw in any other walls; but then I have not been much out of London—only a few times to the sea-side, and never before the time I am going to tell you about at the Farm. As I have said, the sun shone brightly that day, and there were all sorts of sweet scents on the air, from the honeysuckle, and sweetbriar, and the fresh grass, and the bean-fields. The leaves were of such a lovely "tender green," Mamma said; and there were pleasant sounds of lowing cows, and bleating sheep, and the hum of the bees in the bean flowers. Uncle and Aunt Pitt were very glad to see us, and told us we must turn farmers now, and run about in the fields. We had a very nice dinner—a country one, Aunt Pitt said; I thought it much better than a town one, for the chickens were very nice, and the gooseberry-fool and cream better still.

THE COWS.

AFTER dinner, Aunt Pitt said to Cousin George, "I think, my dear, your cousin would like to run about a little while before bed-time. Should you like to see the cows milked, Harry?"

"Yes, Aunt, very much indeed," said I.

"Then go, my dears, and tell Phœbe, the milkmaid, to give you each a glass of fresh warm milk."

Away we all ran, and George took us into a beautiful meadow, all golden with buttercups, in which were seven cows, and a pretty little calf, which was lying down close to its mother, under the shade of a great beech tree. Phœbe was milking one cow, and Tom, the farm man, another. The poor things stood quite still to be milked, and looked very kind and gentle. But that foolish little Annie was afraid to go into the field; and as we could not leave her, we waited at the gate, and looked on till the milking was over. Then George gave Phœbe his mother's message, and she bade us follow her to the dairy, where she gave us each a large cup-full of milk, which tasted quite different from London cows' milk, I assure you; and Phœbe promised us a cup next morning at milking-time.

2

THE POULTRY-YARD.

FROM the pasture, as the green meadow where cows feed is called, we went to the poultry-yard, which Mary said she liked a great deal better than the meadow, and, indeed, it was very amusing. There was an old turkey-cock which strutted about as if he were king of the yard, and gobbled, and tried to frighten me. But George had told me that the old fellow was not really as brave as the cock, so I did not run away, but drove him off. I said to Cousin George, that I thought poultry must be very much like us in some things; for I have noticed that boys who are bullies are generally cowards, like the turkey-cock; while really brave boys are almost always kind and gentle, as the cock seemed to be to the hens and chickens. The geese and ducks, too, were handsome birds. George says a goose ought not to be thought stupid: it is a very sensible creature. One of their geese is quite tame, and follows him about like a dog; whenever he speaks to it, it answers "quack, quack!" I told him what I had read about the geese which saved the Capitol of Rome from being taken by the Gauls, and he liked the story. He says he knows more about animals than books.

3

SHEEP SHEARING.

MARY and Annie went out gathering wild flowers the next day, and met the Shepherd driving all the pretty sheep, which were on the meadow next the house, down to the brook. He stopped and said,

"Would you like to see the sheep-shearing?"

"Oh, yes," said Mary, "very much." So they went with him, and soon afterwards George called me, and said that he was going to take the horses to water, and would I like to go also? I could not manage it just then, because Uncle was showing me the glass beehives, but I said I would follow him soon. By the time I reached the brook, a great many of the poor sheep had lost their wool, and were running and jumping about, looking very bare and naked. But the shearer told Mary that they were glad to be relieved from their heavy coats, which would make them very uncomfortable as the weather grew warmer.

The wool will be sold, and made into cloth, and linseys, and blankets. I do not know what we should do for warm clothes in the winter, if sheep were never sheared.

HAYMAKING.

BUT the greatest fun of our visit to Uncle's Farm was the hay-making. How we tossed about the fresh sweet grass with our prongs and forks, and heaped it up in pretty little piles or hay-cocks! and then we buried each other under it. Mary would not be buried; but while she sat gravely on a haycock, we stole softly behind her, and pulled the hay gently away at the back, and in she sank! Then we tossed it all over her; but she jumped up and shook it off (laughing very good-temperedly, I must say), and threw heaps of it back at us again, and we had a race all over the field, pelting each other. When the hay was quite dry and well made, the men came and carted it, and that was great fun for us boys. The girls and Mamma sat down on the haycocks, and watched us; but they often had to give up their seats and get fresh ones, while we climbed to the top of the load, and helped take up the cocks, and pack them at the top of it, till the waggon was as full as possible.

THE HARVEST.

COUSIN George can use a reaping-hook very cleverly, quite as well as the men. Uncle would not let me try to reap for fear of accidents; but I helped to carry beer to the reapers, and we dined in the field, which was very delightful. Mary and Annie helped the old people glean, and when the last load was carried, we crowned little Annie with a wreath of poppies and blue corn-flowers, tied together with ears of golden wheat, and lifted her on the top of the load, and there George sat and held her quite safely as Queen of the Harvest Home. Uncle kept the feast the next day, not that same evening, and we all went to church, and thanked God for "crowning the year with His goodness," as the Psalm says. The church was decked with flowers and wheat-ears, and looked very pretty, and all the reapers were there with their families, dressed in their Sunday clothes, and looking so happy. After church there was a dinner spread in the meadow under the trees, for the reapers, their wives, and children—roast beef and plum pudding, of course. And they sang songs, and drank healths in Uncle's home-brewed ale, and were very merry.

With the Harvest Home our visit ended; but we hope it will not be long before we go again to stay at my Uncle's Farm.

www.ingramcontent.com/pod-product-compliance
Lightning Source LLC
Chambersburg PA
CBHW021123020726
47500CB00003B/894